Dedication

Obo is dedicated to the memory of my aunt, Alice (Icy) Lent,
who gave me my first set of oil paints.

Acknowledgments

My gratitude goes out to the following individuals who were instrumental in making *Obo* become a reality: Beatrice Oost, who was the first to insist that I do a book; Afolabi Ojumu, who told me the Yoruba word for "monkey"; Willem Langman, age 6, who was the first to test-read the manuscript and provide valuable feedback; and Dominique Anderson, who added encouragement and support when it was needed.

Copyright © 1999
by Bob Anderson

Cover design by Marjoram Productions
Cover art and interior illustrations by Bob Anderson

For information write:
Hampton Roads Publishing Company, Inc.
134 Burgess Lane
Charlottesville, VA 22902

Or call: 804-296-2772
FAX: 804-296-5096
e-mail: hrpc@hrpub.com
Web site: http://www.hrpub.com

If you are unable to order this book from your local bookseller, you may order directly from the publisher.
Quantity discounts for organizations are available.
Call 1-800-766-8009, toll-free.

Library of Congress Catalog Card Number: 98-73916

ISBN 1-57174-124-0

10 9 8 7 6 5 4 3 2 1
Printed on acid-free paper in China

Deep in the rain forest, in the middle of the African continent, there lived a family of monkeys.

The youngest was named Obo.

One day a small, very beautiful bird, unlike any bird the monkey family had ever seen, stopped in to visit.

In spite of its tiny size, the bird had the most remarkable voice. All afternoon it fluttered about amongst the monkey troop and sang some of the sweetest songs the monkeys had ever heard.

Finally, as the day was drawing to a close, the bird said, "Well, I must be off now. My family is certain to be wondering where I am."

"Wait!" the monkeys called out, "Before you go, please tell us where you come from."

"I come from Paradise," the bird answered. Then, as the sun began to set, he flew off, the lovely sound of his song trailing behind him.

When Obo asked the older monkeys where Paradise was, they said that they had no idea.

As time went on, Obo couldn't get the sweet sounds of the bird's songs out of his head, so, as soon as he was old enough to go off into the jungle on his own, he decided that he would leave his family and friends to search for Paradise.

He started off in the same direction that he remembered the bird had taken when he left.

Obo hadn't gone far when he came across a serval. Thinking the serval might be of some help, Obo asked, "Excuse me, Mr. Serval, have you ever heard of a place called Paradise?"

"What's that?" the serval asked. He had been following a lizard and seemed annoyed at the distraction caused by Obo's appearance. "Why don't you come a little closer. I didn't quite hear you."

Knowing that it wasn't a good idea for monkeys to get too close to servals, Obo replied, "Oh, no, no, no. I think I'll just go find someone else to ask." And Obo moved on.

Feeling thirsty after a hard day of traveling, Obo dropped down to a jungle pool to get a drink. He had taken only a few sips when he noticed a movement nearby that seemed to cause little ripples in the water. He looked up and saw two big bubble-shaped objects that appeared to be floating on the surface of the pool just in front of him. When Obo realized that he was looking right into the two eyes of a big, long-nosed crocodile, he quickly jumped back into the trees above.

"Why, it's Mr. Crocodile!" Obo exclaimed. "Have you ever heard of a place called Paradise?"

"Come on back down by my pool," the crocodile replied, "and I'll tell you what I know about Paradise."

"Oh, no, no, no. I think I'll just go find someone else to ask," said Obo. And he moved on.

Continuing his journey, Obo came across two okapis, who were quietly grazing in a dense area of the forest. They were so quiet and their colors and skin patterns looked so much like the plants and vines around them, that Obo almost didn't see them. Obo knew that okapis were some of the most peaceful creatures in the jungle, so he went right up to them to find out if they were familiar with a place called Paradise.

"Paradise?" asked one of the okapis. "Hmm, we're so content here with all this good food and quiet shade. Why, we're really not interested in thinking much about other places. Nope. Afraid we can't help you there, little buddy."

"Well, thanks anyway," said Obo. And he moved on.

Shortly afterward, Obo ran across a warthog. "Aha," thought Obo, "warthogs are always snorting about all over the jungle. I'll bet he knows something about Paradise."

"Oh, Mr. Warthog," Obo called out. "Can you tell me anything about a place called Paradise?"

"Get lost!" the warthog grunted. "Can't you see I'm about to take a nice mud bath?" And the warthog turned his back on Obo and wallowed into a most disgusting-looking mud hole.

"I'll bet that's his tenth mud bath of the day," sighed Obo. "Oh well, I guess I'll just move on and ask someone else." And Obo moved on.

Sometime later, Obo saw a group of baboons, and, knowing that they were distant cousins, he assumed that they might be a little more sociable than the warthog. But he was wrong.

When Obo asked the biggest baboon if he knew where Paradise was, the baboon just laughed. "Go back up into your treetop, you funny looking little thing," he said. Then the rest of the baboons joined in laughing at Obo, and some even started to throw small sticks at him.

Obo was shocked. "Such behavior! And coming from creatures who are actually distant relatives of mine. Why, you're even ruder than that nasty old warthog!" And Obo moved on.

BABOONS YANKARI
BOB ANDERSON MAY 91

Nearby, Obo saw a leopard. Now, leopards are even more dangerous than servals, as any monkey would know. But Obo thought he would approach the leopard anyway, just in case he might be of some help.

When Obo asked his question, the leopard said he was looking for baboons. But he was at least polite enough to tell Obo that he didn't know anything about a place called Paradise. The leopard did, however, suggest that Obo look for his two cousins, the black panthers, who were resting in a grove of rubber trees. Obo thanked the leopard and told him where he might find some baboons.

It wasn't too difficult for Obo to find the black panthers, but, knowing that they were just a black version of a leopard, he kept his distance.

"Hey, you black panthers down there," he called out. The panthers looked up to see Obo swinging from a vine above. "I'm looking for a place called Paradise, and your cousin, the leopard, suggested that I stop by here and get directions from you. Do you know where I can find it?"

The panthers told Obo they remembered a place called Paradise being discussed by some of the animals who lived on the other side of the savannah. They told him which way to go, but then suggested that Obo drop down out of the trees and come a little closer.

"Oh, no, no, no," said Obo. "You've been very kind to give me what information you have. I think I'll just move on."

Obo didn't like savannahs, because there was too much open space and not enough trees where a monkey like Obo would be safe. "Well," he thought to himself, "If I'm ever going to continue my search, I guess I'll just have to take the chance and go down to the ground."

He was just about to drop down into the grass when a large lion appeared. "Yikes!" yelled Obo, and he jumped back up into the trees. "Hi there, Mr. Lion! Ah, ca-can you tell me where to find a place called Paradise?"

"Paradise?" the lion asked. "Never heard of it," he roared. "Probably doesn't even exist. If it did, I certainly would have heard of it. Why, I'm the king. I know everything. Say there, little fella, come down here so I can get a better look at you."

"Oh, no, no, no. I think I'll just go find someone else to ask." And Obo moved on.

Obo finally found a string of trees that were close enough together that he was able to travel from tree to tree without having to scurry across the open ground.

He gradually made his way out to the middle of the savannah, where he found three giraffes. When he mentioned his quest, one of them said that they had heard the "Old Wise One" mention Paradise. They suggested that Obo try to find the Old Wise One.

The Old Wise One! Obo became excited. This was the first solid clue that he had received. He began to move faster, asking every creature he came across if they knew of the place called Paradise or if they knew of someone called the Old Wise One.

A little farther on, a gazelle, who was resting under a tree, said that she didn't know Paradise, but that she did know the Old Wise One. She hadn't seen the Old Wise One for several years, but she suggested that Obo go toward the place where the sun sets at night.

Obo took the gazelle's advice and moved off toward the place where the sun sets at night.

After traveling for what seemed to be a terribly long time, he reached the end of the savannah and came to another forest, which led to some mountains. On the side of one of the mountains, Obo ran into another set of distant cousins, the gorillas. These were a lot friendlier than the baboon cousins. They not only told him which direction to go to find the Old Wise One, but they also told him where he might find some bananas.

Since the bananas were in the same direction that the gorillas had said the Old Wise One had last taken, Obo decided to stop for a nice snack before continuing his journey.

As he approached the banana grove, Obo met a woman walking through the forest with her child. She told him which direction he might go to find the Old Wise One. But she suggested that he stay away from the banana grove, since it had been planted by her husband, who did not like anyone taking his bananas without permission. She did give him one banana, for which he was grateful.

Obo said thank you and moved on.

Obo came to a river and began to follow it. Obo traveled on and on, swinging from branch to vine, and vine to branch, keeping close to the river and stopping time and again to question anyone he could find. Several days had gone by like this when it occurred to Obo that this neighborhood looked very familiar.

When he came upon a family of pygmy hippos, Obo recognized them and realized that his travels had taken him in a big circle. He was actually very close to his own home.

Poor Obo had traveled for such a long time, searching practically every corner of the jungle, plus the mountains and the savannah, only to end up back where he had started. He felt disappointed to have gone so far and to have had so little success. "Oh well," he thought, "one never knows. I might as well ask the pygmy hippos if they know anything."

When asked whether or not they knew where to find the Old Wise One, one of the pygmy hippos answered, "Why yes, she just passed by this way with her son. There they are now! They just crossed the river and are entering the forest on the other side."

Obo couldn't believe it! He looked across the river and was just able to catch a glimpse of two forest elephants disappearing into the thick jungle. One of them was full of long, sagging wrinkles and appeared to be much older than the other. She must be the Old Wise One!

One of the pygmy hippos gave him a ride across the river, and Obo was off in hot pursuit.

"Are you the Old Wise One?" he asked, once he had caught up with the elephant at a clearing. "Yes," said the old forest elephant.

"Have you ever heard of a place called Paradise?" asked Obo.

"Of course I have," answered the Old Wise One.

"Well," gasped the excited monkey, "I must find it. Please, ma'am, tell me where it is."

The Old Wise One laughed and said, "Why, it's here. This is Paradise. Didn't you know? Paradise is exactly where you think it is."

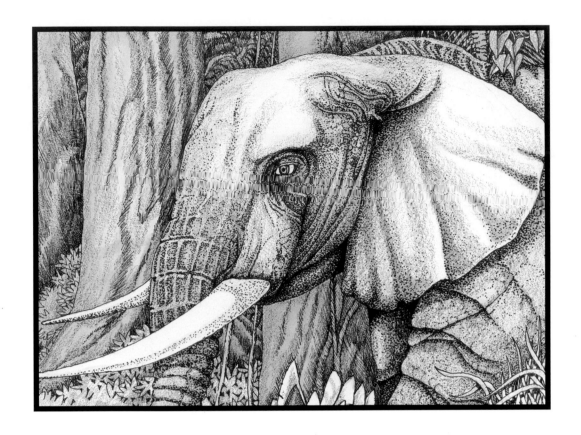

Obo blinked and asked again, "I don't think I understood you correctly. I'm looking for a place called Paradise. Did you say that this is Paradise?"

"Yes," said the Old Wise One. "Open your eyes and look around you."

Just then, Obo heard a sweet song floating over the jungle. It was the song he had heard so long ago from the beautiful little song bird. He blinked again and looked around. The bird flew up to him, still singing, and landed on a branch.

"It's the bird!" Obo exclaimed. He blinked a third time, and, when he opened his eyes, he could see that the bird had a bright red beak with red feathers on his cheeks and a tail with stripes like a zebra.

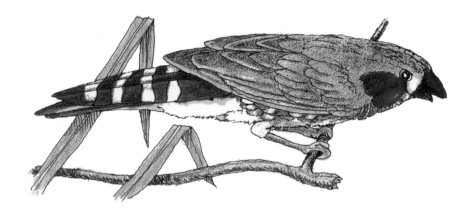

Obo looked back at the Old Wise One and noticed that several other elephants had moved into the clearing. The elephants started making trumpet-like sounds as they began to sing along with the bird.

Suddenly, another sound joined in. A herd of hippos, then some rhinos, then some water buffalo—all snorting and making sounds that, when all linked together with the bird's and the elephants' songs, sounded like a small band.

Soon the clearing began to fill up with all sorts of creatures, each one making his or her own special sound and each adding to the music that the small bird had started. What had begun as a simple song had now grown into a symphony.

Obo closed his eyes for a minute, and a light breeze started up. He sniffed the air and smelled the natural perfumes of the flowers. Then he heard a familiar noise coming from high up in the canopy of the forest. It was his own family. "I'm home," he said. "Yes, this must be Paradise."

Glossary

Greet the dik-dik, meet the monkey, and get to know the gnu. There are thirty different animal species in the picture of the African waterhole—ninety-nine animals altogether. Can you spot them all? Discover new animal friends by matching the pictures below to the drawing on pages 38 and 39.

baboon: (ba-'bün) baboons travel in large, organized groups and are considered highly intelligent. There are five species, ranging in size from thirty to ninety pounds (the males are twice the size of females).

boomslang: ('büm-slaŋ) an extremely venomous tree snake whose variable body color makes it hard to see.

black rhinoceros: ('blak rī-'nä-sə-rəs) the smaller, but more aggressive, of two African species of rhinoceros. A rhinoceros is a large, powerful, plant-eating animal with one or two horns on its snout.

Cape buffalo: ('kāp 'bəf-ə-,lō) also known as the African buffalo, is larger than the Indian water buffalo, has never been domesticated, and is considered by some as the most dangerous animal in the world for man.

casqued hornbill: ('kaskd 'horn-bil) one of several species of hornbills found in Africa. Hornbills are known for their enormous bills.

cinnamon chested bee eater: ('si-nə-mən 'ches-təd 'bē 'ēt-er) a small, eight-inch-long, East African bird that eats bees and lives in forests.

crocodile: ('krä-kə-,dīl) of the twelve species of crocodile, the most common found in Africa are the dwarf—which grow to only five feet—the long-nose, and the Nile, which grow to twenty-two feet and are the most dangerous to man.

crocodile bird: ('krä-kə-,dīl 'bərd)) a small bird that picks ticks and other external parasites off of the hides crocodiles, also known as the "black-backed courser."

crowned crane: ('kraund 'krān) a tall bird with a decorative crown found in East and South Africa.

dik-dik: ('dik-'dik) a very small—twelve to sixteen inches high at the shoulder—African antelope, named for the sound it makes when alarmed.

duck: ('dək) a speckled African duck. A number of species of ducks commonly migrate between Europe and Africa. This is a speckled duck that lives at the National Zoo.

elephant: ('e-lə-fənt) the African bush elephant and the pygmy or "forest" elephant are two different varieties of the same species, even though the forest elephant can be half the size of a typical bush elephant.

gerenuk: ('gĕr-ə-'noōk) an African antelope that often stands on its hind legs to eat leaves from high bushes and trees.

giraffe: (jə-'raf) the tallest of all animals, can grow to eighteen feet in height. Their closest relative is the okapi.

gnu: ('nü) also known as a wildebeest, an antelope found in large herds in east and south Africa.

goliath frog: (gə-lī 'eth frôg) the largest frog in the world, growing to twelve inches and able to jump fourteen feet. Africa also has the smallest frog in the world (one inch), the phrynobatrachus chitialaenis.

gorilla: (gə-'ri-lə) the largest of all anthropoids (man-like apes), a large male can weigh up to 390 pounds.

guenon monkey: ('gwē-nən 'məŋ-kē) one of the most common tree-dwelling rain forest monkeys in Africa. Obo is a spot-nose guenon. There are about twenty species, only two of which are ground-dwellers.

hippopotamus: (,hip-ə-'pä-tə-məs) can grow to fifteen feet in length and up to 9,000 pounds. Hippos live in herds and spend most of their time in the water.

ibis: ('ī-bəs) a wading bird that eats fish and builds nests in bushes and trees adjacent to lakes and rivers. Ibises occur in all warm regions of the world except the South Pacific Islands.

kob: (′käb) one of six species of African "kobus" antelopes.

kudu: (′küd-ü) a large antelope found in South Africa and Rhodesia.

leopard: (′lə-pərd) has the widest range of any of the big cats, including much of Asia, the Arabian Peninsula, northeast Africa, and all of Africa south of the Sahara Desert.

lesser flamingo: (′le-sər fla-′mĭŋgō) one of four species of flamingo, this species is the most common and can be found in East Africa and India.

lion: (one lioness and two lions) (′lī-ən) the proverbial "king of beasts" is one of the best known of all animals. Lions once occupied all of Africa—except for the Sahara Desert—much of Asia, and some areas of Europe. Today the only wild lions are in Africa, with the exception of about three hundred that are protected in a park in India.

old world white pelican: (′old ′wərld ′hwīt ′pə-li-kən) similar to pelicans found in America but found more in fresh-water lakes and lagoons in Africa.

potto: (′pät-o) a small, slow-moving, tree-dwelling, nocturnal, tropical African primate. Also known as a "bush bear," "tree bear," and a "softly-softly."

pygmy hippo: (′pig-mē ′hi-pō) much smaller than regular hippos. Pygmy hippos tend to spend more time on land than in water, as do their bigger relatives.

spotted hyena: (′spät-ed hī-′ē-nə) a scavanger that often lives on the leftovers from other meat-eaters. The spotted hyena is the largest and most common of three species of hyena.

zebra: (′zē-brə) there are three species of zebra, and since I drew these from my imagination they don't accurately correspond to any of the species, although they resemble the Burchell's zebra a little more than the Grevy's or mountain zebras.

Along the way, before you arrived at the waterhole, you saw other creatures who live in Paradise. Now it's time to meet them . . .

 **black panther:** (ˈblak ˈpan-thər) a leopard whose background color is black instead of yellow. Sometimes you can still see the spots on a black leopard (panther).

 **gazelle:** (ga-ˈzəl) any number of small, graceful, and swift African and Asiatic antelopes noted for their soft lustrous eyes.

 **okapi:** (ō-ˈkäp-ē) an African mammal related to the giraffe but with shorter neck and legs. Females, which are larger than males, grow to about five feet at the shoulder. These animals are very secretive, inhabit dense rain forests of the Congo, and were unknown to science until 1900.

 **serval:** (ˈsər-vəl) a long-legged African wildcat having large untufted ears and a tawny black spotted coat. Servals are very quick. They can run and climb and they inhabit both savannahs and bushy forest in most areas south of the Sahara Desert but north of the equator.

 **warthog:** (ˈwȯrt-ˌhȯg) a very common African wild hog with two pairs of warty growths on the face and large protruding tusks.

 zebra finch: (ˈzēb-rə ˈfinch) a small, colorful songbird having a short, stout cone-shaped bill good for crushing seeds.

Ready for your own adventures? Receive a free 17" x 22" color poster of the African waterhole scene by writing to: Obo Poster, Hampton Roads Publishing Company, 134 Burgess Lane, Charlottesville, VA 22902. Include $2.95 for shipping and handling. Available while supply lasts.

Author's Notes

Obo is the Yoruba word for monkey. Since it is also the author's name "turned inside out," it seemed an appropriate name for the story's main character.

The monkey, Obo, is a Spot-Nose Guenon, a small monkey with a very distinctive nose that inhabits the tops of trees in most of the rain forest areas of Africa.

The bird who tells Obo about paradise is a Zebra Finch, a small colorful bird with bright chestnut cheeks. Zebra Finches live in Australia, though, not Africa, which would explain why the monkeys were unfamiliar with it. They are commonly raised in captivity as caged songbirds. The bird in the story must have been a caged bird which escaped!

Certain environmental and habitational inaccuracies in the illustrations should be pointed out. The pygmy hippos, which I have drawn in a group or small herd, are really solitary animals, which inhabit swamps and waterways in the Ivory Coast, West Africa, and, unlike their larger, more common hippopotamus cousins, pygmy hippos never travel or live in groups. The models for these pygmy hippos all live at the National Zoo in Washington, D.C. I liked them so much that I couldn't stop drawing them—until I ended up with a herd.

When a friend who was reading this story came to the part about the black panthers, he said that he thought rubber trees were from South America and didn't really occur in Africa. I actually did this drawing while I was in West Africa. I never did find out whether the rubber trees I saw there were imported from South America for cultivation or were some other species of rubber tree-like plant that were native to West Africa. In any case, the rubber plants are not an inaccuracy (although the drawing itself is a fantasy).

Another inaccuracy should be pretty easy to figure out. The last illustration in the story shows a gathering of animals at a water hole. Many of these creatures would never be found in the same location together. There are a total of ninety-nine creatures in this drawing.

All of the drawings in Obo were originally done in pen and ink. I added color with magic markers and colored pencils because of the difficulty some young children have in focusing on the intricate details of my drawings. After you've found all of the hidden animals in each drawing, see if you can find all ninety-nine in the last drawing.

Young
Spirit
Books

Hampton Roads Publishing Company is dedicated to providing quality children's books that stimulate the intellect, teach valuable lessons, and allow our children's spirits to grow. We have created our line of *Young Spirit Books* for the evolving human spirit of our children. Give your children *Young Spirit Books*—their key to a whole new world!

Hampton Roads Publishing Company
publishes books on a variety of subjects including
metaphysics, health, complementary medicine, visionary fiction,
and other related topics. For a copy of our latest catalog,
call toll-free (800) 766-8009, or send your name and address to

Hampton Roads Publishing Company, Inc.
134 Burgess Lane
Charlottesville, VA 22902
e-mail: hrpc@hrpub.com
www.hrpub.com